Lucky's Pup Pal

by Macy Rushing

Char Char Bean books

an imprint of
Rope Swing Publishing

Paperback ISBN: 978-1-954058-35-4

Copyright © 2022
Written by: Macy Rushing
Design by: Rope Swing Publishing, LLC
Illustration elements by: Amalie Roepstorff, Claudia Pisoineri-Mesteru, Star Brite
Designs, and Star Jam for Kids

Published by: CharChar Bean books, a children's imprint of Rope Swing Publishing, LLC

To my parents!
They may have feared
what animal I would
bring home next, but
they supported me
through it all!
Love y'all dearly!

There are so many different animals that live on the farm and my mom loves adding new babies to the family.

One day I remember her coming home with a tiny ball of fur. I couldn't tell exactly what it was, until I got closer.

It was a puppy! I love puppies; they are so playful, and I couldn't wait to meet him. When she introduced him to me he smelled awful.

She told me, Dad, and the rest of the family that she'd found him abandoned at the gas station. I guess that's why she named him Diesel.

My family must have good luck with gas stations because that's where mama and dad met.

Diesel would run up to the fence and just stare at me. Every time I tried to get close he would run off, and I wasn't sure why.

Then I realized it was because I was so much bigger than the other fur animals. I guess he'd never seen something as big as me before.

I was scaring him and didn't even mean too. That's the last thing I want to do is scare anyone, especially a fur friend who needs us.

After he grew up to be a big dog, we got much closer. I guess he realized even though I'm big, I am also gentle.

He visits me and the other fur friends daily, sometimes more than my sisters visit, but that's okay I know they have school.

Diesel is the farms guard dog. He runs all the bad animals away, like hogs, foxes, deer and sometimes even coyotes. Those are really scary.

Now, on hot days, Diesel will get in the pond with the horses and me. It's the best way to cool off. It sure gets hot in Louisiana.

During the winter, it gets so cold that Diesel will go inside the house with Mama, and Dad puts me in a warm stall in the barn to keep me from freezing.

Guess I am way too big to go inside. Plus, I am not house trained like Diesel. Boy, wouldn't that be a big mess?

One time during really bad weather, it was lightening and thundering. Diesel got scared and ran off into the woods.

I remember Mama calling his name and looking for him. She asked if I knew where he was, but I wasn't sure. I could tell she was worried about him.

Thankfully, once the weather stopped he returned home. We all were so glad!

The farm wouldn't be the same if we didn't have our sweet, Diesel.

Made in the USA
Middletown, DE
18 April 2023

29045937R00015